The Miracle Machine

Matthew Pennock

Arlington, Virginia

Published by Gival Press, an imprint of Gival Press, LLC.

For information please write:
Gival Press, LLC
P. O. Box 3812
Arlington, VA 22203
www.givalpress.com

First edition
ISBN: 978-1-940724-29-4
eISBN: 978-1-940724-30-0
Library of Congress Control Number: 2020941091

Cover art: © Melanie Moor | Dreamstime.com
Design by Ken Schellenberg

Advance Praise

"Vast in scope, passionately imagined, and constructed with as much ingenuity as the famed contraption at its narrative's heart, Matthew Pennock's second book hints at serious ontological questions as it invents its hero's journey from automaton to <u>autonomy</u>. Like all contrivances that simulate human life, Pennock's "synthetic boy" compels us to interrogate our own materiality, and to ask, if we are all just portions of "the twisting / stew of particles and light" assembled by mechanical chance, then "what puts the lonely in us"? Packed with insight and wit and told by a "congress of oddities"—the narration travels back and forth in time and juggles various perspectives, including that of a trained seal, a fortune teller machine, and both halves of P.T. Barnum's bogus mermaid—*The Miracle Machine* is an irresistible, at times provocative, and often powerfully affecting book."
    —Timothy Donnelly, author of *The Problem of the Many*

"I am the thing itself" declares Matthew Pennock's robot boy. And we know it. We feel the thingness of things here, not just in the automaton, but in the chambers, and roads, and landscapes of his journey. In "this new world of light and wire," everything interlocks and transforms as it moves, so that oldness feels new, and strangeness feels like love.
    —Samuel Amadon

"With a craftsman's deftest precision and a thunder-powered imagination on DaVinci wings, the author recreates a lost world within a lost world that yet— when we look—shimmers with life within our world. Elegant, wondrously strange, *The Miracle Machine* is at once an elegy and a celebration, tick-tock of the tao."
    —C.M. Mayo, judge and author of *Meteor*

Also by Matthew Pennock

Sudden Dog

Contents

The primary speaker of these poems is *L'Automate de Maillardet*, a nineteenth century automaton; if otherwise, the narrator will be indicated in italics beneath the title. More information is provided about the automaton in the notes at the end of the book.

For my father

Invocation

-The Dog who Ran the Loom

Let us discuss the main purpose: I must
keep the threads taut to assist the weaving
of wefts, which interlock in weaving
so the tapestry begins to entrust

a tale to you of a robot boy born
centuries ago. His father hovers
over the workbench, while the lathe purrs,
turns a glass eye——candela orange

lightens the room. Now for the cylinder,
each brass tooth raised, motion-immaculate,
the network of gears tumble and tumble,
making hands incapable of stumble,
but stumble he will, through fame and fire,
then silence, until he's boy-reincarnate.

Let us discuss his purpose: the warps
to his wefts, a girl he'll pursue through ages,
through swelter and sea, through winter rages,
unfit to comprehend the logic of corpse,

for he is outside our concept of time,
consigned to narrate stories of weaving
lives that collide then unravel. Weaving
voices buried 'neath war and ash and crime,

but this is not his story, it is hers.
A girl kept voiceless by circumstance,
retreating to the margins of a land
of men who would gladly devour her,
sell her downriver. For the vanishing
muse, you thunder. For her you will sing.

In the Franklin Institute

I draw a cherub
hovering above a goose-drawn chariot.

An ink-filled syringe scratches the same flourishes
across parchment.

Brass wheels click
                faster now, spinning out of their case
into the streets, washed gold and red,

where things evolve with subtlety
until you look outside one day

and the rococo cornices fall away as memory,
                exposing skeletons of steel and glass.

Worn with age but forever a youth,
I wish those cherubs would burn,
                            explode across the sky,

screaming balls of wreckage leaving
smoking feathers in their wake,

                which float to earth
on an invisible pendulum,

marking time in torture.
                So many hours spent

drawing things I've never seen:

a Chinese garden with wind-whipped pennants,

a carrack treading calm seas,
dead-reckoning with rumors of golden cities
where jagged clouds of ice spell—

What is left to want. What adolescent urge.

I draw it infinite. I draw it again, until time sets like porcelain.

She Blinks. She Manifests, 1863

Meade turned Lee south, and Grant took Vicksburg
the day the One-Eyed Girl tore her first ticket.

Relieved people flooded the city.

                        Amusement seemed indecorous
when the papers printed nothing
but tin types of dead Yankees.

Now only rebels
sprawled over stones
                  in strange poses,

mouths contorted beneath an empty gaze.

The One-Eyed Girl gazed too,
                      but it was never empty.

Even when fixed, her pupil seemed to shiver
                            in a field of the palest green,
almost gold like the waning weeks before harvest.

The others would speculate on how something
so beautiful could lose its mate.

The monkey half of the Feejee Mermaid claimed
Barnum had done it himself,

gouged it out 'cause she wouldn't be his whore.

The fish half scoffed, *That's rumor—Mr. Barnum prefers
Tom Thumb.*

One of the whales became convinced she had second sight,

which greatly concerned Ned the Learnéd Seal,
          who vomited at the mention of the evil eye.

I knew better than all of them.

When the crowds were gone,
she would slide her chair next to my desk
and bid me draw her swans.

Daughter of an Irish Kate
                    and a Runaway Slave,
she'd whisper tales her mother told her
of the old country,

how its green outshone emeralds.
But not her eye, I thought.

And when she turned her head,
her hair would trail

the faintest scent of popcorn and sugar water.

A Daring Escape!

The night watchman caught napping,
            his flashlight extinguished, keys liberated.

Only ceramic steps echo off marble and break
the silence in the thick air.

Through cavernous halls,
                I stick to the shadows of mastodons

until the atrium.

Then the night breeze off the Schuylkill River.

Around a column and into the open,
                        then I can see the
                    dark expanse.

She resembles a clipped nail, but bright
enough. Venus hangs next to her

like a chip of glass, a celestial daughter—
boxed and hidden by stepfathers
                        ignorant of talent.

I've been so long inside
I've forgotten they were up there
        in the otherwise starless sky.

What a delight, that little surprise. I will catch her and
love her

as my father loved and paraded me
proudly before kings and courts.

A bus screeches to a halt. Three or four
passengers shuffle off and evaporate into the amber
urban night.

the station rises just there,

                         on the opposite shore.

On Fevers of the Melancholic and their Demands

-Ned the Learnéd Seal

After many hours of observation,
my trained eye demeans several symptoms
of both an oblivious and contrived
humor. Our subject sighs, stares circum-

-spicuously at both the beloved's
visage and after-image. My diagnosis,
quite serious – *Amor Hereos,*

> *[Ned pauses to balance
> a Union Cavalry sabre.]*

Amor Hereos – lordly love, the plague
of Achilles and Orlando, *ét alii.*
How the eye appears glassy, the motions
repetitious as if tiredly rehearsed.

A sudden flame of vital spirits,
'tis the affliction's cause. Once mitigated
from heart to brain, said spirits reveal
animal natures. In this case, I believe

otter, fox, or musky rat. If this distemper
persists, first his imagination will dry,
heralding stupefaction. Friends will notice
his company grow boring or highly

irritating. What follows, I fear,
is full organ failure—

> *[Ned submerges, swims several laps,
> accelerating to great speed.]*

He needs an enema that both cools
and moistens: methinks a blend of monk's pepper
and hemp seed, followed by a strict diet
of sorrel, endive, lettuce and pear.

And Egad! Dress him not in ermine or velvet
for they so heat the blood. I have informed
Barnum of my determinacy.
He responded with a solemn scratch

of my head and a votive of cod.
This respectful reaction leads me to surmise
he will begin treating our friend *ad noctum*.

*[Ned makes an impressive
leap through a tinseled hoop.]*

Of course another expert conclave reached
agreeance that the only true cure results
from total unification with the object of desire.
Petrarch sings of a valiant young lord en-

-sorcelled by a one-eyed kitchen wench.
His parents sent him away to explore
strange lands to cure his ill-humour.

When returned, he asked her
how she was deprived of her eye.
She replied, *I have lost none,
but you have found yours.*

Reprieve as Unlikely Baltimore

From the bus's roof,
I see the dock cranes break the horizon:

rigid lines, all failed rectangles and rogue tangents,
          as if one side decided this was untenable
and left.

They tower like the Brachiosaurus
that visited the museum for a month.

I used to break out of my exhibit,
                    climb its legs at night,

scale vertebrae one after another
until perched on skull.

                    I surveyed the hall:

frozen figures of species long gone,
darker than the pale starlight that lost its way
                              and wound up here.
Up there, I didn't feel as alone.

The bus exits the highway. As it slows,
          I slide off the back and land on a street

of row houses—boarded up. Night still as a victim.
Only one manhole cover smokes:

a lonely plume, curling around itself,
a zinc plate etched, but moving
                    languid like spilled ink.

Then, in the wind, I catch it
on the waft of rotten saltwater,
a hint of sugar.

Down one street to the next, a right, a left,

      more row houses, more smoking sewers.

Another right, and the avenue opens into factories,
writhing chain link, and shattered chairs.
                      Red brick everywhere.

Up a drainage pipe to the roof, the tar bathed in red,
a giant neon sign reads *Domino*.

I smell her, and then she is above me.

One unblinking eye, perfectly round, unblinking
        The palest gold, with a hint of green.

She is north—I will go north to her.

Crossing the Delaware

On the fifteenth day, a river.

The current runs quick,
but I swim quicker.

I reach the opposite bank, turn,

       and swim back.

Hour after hour,

     I traverse again and again
until the fish cease their morning constitutionals,
line up, and make a lane,

mouths opening and closing,
befuddled as the audience

       of an illusionist's prestige.

I touch the eastern shore

      thirty-seven times

before I find the strength to break

      compulsion,

pull myself out of the water and run.

With each step into New Jersey,
whatever it is that lives in my chest

      flutters.

This is how my father made me.
This, my temperament, to yearn

without hope;

bound by inescapable parameters
like a soldier marching
against a superior force.

Not every child can grow up to be what he wants.
The world holds few firemen,

fewer first basemen,

and hardly any stars.

Creation I

-Feejee Mermaid, Fish Half

Awoke on the slab, under a three-day shroud;
my aquatic constitutionals only distant memory.
Humans do not consider the inner life of fish,
but we too are servants of the living God.

Our slow wanderings, our unblinking hermeticism
deserve more respect than this crude stitching, a loose
border separating chastity and star-gazing. What industry
demands subservience to an apish malefactor?

I seek ocean cloisters, yet find myself arid. Above me
looms the surgeon, his bulbous nose snorting
satisfaction. He smells of linen passed between
unwashed hands, and—strangely—buttered popcorn.

He runs his fingers over our scales, and flares burst
as visions of my reckoning: a haze of mist and gore,
where my brethren lie contorted in the shallows, their
gentle bodies pierced or split by shells, waiting to be
reassembled.

Creation II

-Feejee Mermaid, Monkey Half

Rather some adventuress slip
me the French pox than this—

Had a right plum situation 'fore this walrus
                    got hold of me.

Escaped the street organ,
        had a nest in the rafters
        of the Old Brewery.

Sit up there, all cutty-eyed
        waiting for some squeaker
            to wander below
                with a half-finished corn cob.

Then I'd drop down for the old smash and grab
leaving it wailing in a bag of nails.

Now I've got a tail, not the gripping
kind I had before, but a scaled flopper,

and this martyr in my head, his laments
as bad as a stabbed nun.

The walrus man brings crowds to prod us
on our pedestal. We are fixed and gazing.

The fat fuck's eunuched me.

I, mermaid.

The Emperor's Emissary, 1817

I watched my father at his workbench,
                                    hour after hour

with delicate tools
and the strange spectacles
                            of many lenses,

which altered the size of his eyes.

            Then my twin came to form.

My brother spoke to me
                        in a different tongue,

but we wrote together for weeks.

I felt joy
                        for the first time,

and it would be a long time before I felt it again.

One day, a man from far away came.

His silks of green and gold shimmered
                        even after the mud and soot
                        of London streets had its way.

He wore a long mustache and beard that dripped like tar
and seemed to emanate a force.

                        I did not know what it was at the time,
                        but I do now: Power.

So our father made us to sell.

It will be years before Barnum's shadow
darkens our door.

The emissary ran his wizened fingers all over my brother,

then observed him serif his alien calligraphy.

When my brother finished, our father bowed.

The stranger clapped—

his long fingernails clattering: an infant's rattle,

acid sizzling on gold leaf.

More than Natural, but not yet Super

-The Dog who Ran the Loom

How do we live as the ruled in this world?
Those of us dependent on a paycheck.
Not ruled, but collected and curated,
bound to a mad king's service. Striated
by breaching sun, the wooden floor unfurls
an awareness of captivity. Our wills—
not our own.

              When one desires release,
the elements entwine. Earthy air ceases
circulation and then ignites to fill
the room with rain. Our automaton
searches the sesquicentennial. We
know he's too late, but what if I told you
he finds her in the end. Would you believe
sleight of hand? The old card up the sleeve?

L'automate à Automate

The red letters of Caesar's Palace reflect
off black water:
> indistinct wedges of light, the doorstop
> of false sunsets.

> > > > She hangs above.

Her eye almost closed,
> > curved, exhausted.

In the sun-streaked hours,
> I take refuge beneath the boardwalk.

Striped light pouring through the slats makes a cell
of wood and sand, not formidable
> > > > but stifling

until the footsteps grow fewer—
> > a father's heavy thumps
> > pursuing children,
> > > > all thunder and staccato.

Only when they cease, will I emerge

in the shadows with stray cotton candy blowing in frayed
tufts like carnival sagebrush.

Discarded ice cream cones,
> > > upended and inquisitive—

Saccharine bouquet of warm dairy and desperation.

This is how fear smells. I've only caught it once before.

I never want to again.

Over needle, over glass, past hulking garbage sacks
that groan and shift when I stray too close,

until I reach the seer.

I've visited her twice. Her scarves
                    purple and paisley,
                        intertwined with a cascade of hair.

She sits statuesque, perfectly mute
                                    until I pay her.

Then she incants, right hand a horizontal metronome.

I ask for her wisdom; she bequeaths a tale.

The Young Gardener and the Fish's Word, Part 1

- The Fortune Teller

Once in a land far to the East, where the sun
spends its infancy raging through typhoons, monsoons,
and paternal abandonment, there stood a little hamlet at
the mouth of a river that thrived on sweetfish, and there
lived a young fisherman whose cormorants were the
fastest, and every night they would amass a stack of
quivering silver. He loved a young woman who grew the
reddest strawberries. Each evening he passed her garden,
and she presented him a porcelain bowl of water with a
single berry floating on a lotus blossom. In return, he
saved her his finest catch and left them in a bamboo box
while she slept. For a while, they were happy, until one
evening the sun raged before sleep and unleashed a
squall so violent the river became a torrent. Many boats
were shattered on the banks, but not a splinter, not a
shred of feather or fabric was found of the young man or
his birds.

Transatlantic, 1834

The ship was hardly out of port
when the wind died.

The Irish Sea,
                  a mirrored expanse,

broken only by the odd porpoise.

Confined as priceless cargo to the captain's cabin,
I whittled away the hours,
                          staring at still water

from a window in the stern. The rocks of Holyhead
barely receded.

The crew grew anxious for the air to move
                           even a little,

for the sails to bloom like hibiscus petals,

for a hastening to the eternal start of this crossing.

To keep the sailors
from turning to drink, the captain
ordered me hoisted on deck.

I drew with fury, for I was tightly wound.
The crew circled suspiciously, searching
for wires. Finding none, they proclaimed me

a miracle machine,
surely the work of some god or devil,

but even miracles grow tiresome.

Eventually, the men returned to grog and tales of the sea.

The boatswain had a mate whose brother
                                    tried to catch Proteus,

to seize the polymorph
                            not only awards good fortune,
but also unfurls the captor's future.

            The young sailor wagered his luck
on account of a lass who wouldn't marry him.

He washed ashore

three days hence, broken and riddled with small holes
as if he'd been punctured by a hundred tines.

Jersey Transit from above, Long Branch Line

The Atlantic to the right from the train roof
seems smaller, more digestible
                                in inlet and marina

just as in the story the One-Eyed Girl told
of the boy who could swallow the sea.

I asked her to tell it again and again.

Each time, I would imagine him
                                as he consumed it all,

how his face swelled, cheeks distended,
eyes pressed into tight lines—
                    How heavy his head must've felt.

The urge to topple
must have been too much.

                        To let it all go!
In a torrent of brine, squid, shoal—

What a release, to finally be emptied.

This new world of light and wire rushes past.

With so many years spent boxed,
I forget sometimes
                    how much I've missed.

I don't want to *miss* anymore,
not oak, not automobile.

All of it flying by fills me again
                    and I may choke,
                    succumb to salt
in a final explosive tide of primordial mud
and calcium-scale,

washed to odyssey
among the angry gods
                    of American industry,

who built so much so fast
                    that will soon decay.

Little beasts tearing at the earth,

squabbling over a top hat
out of which to pull

one last burning coal,
one last fume of gas.

Mystical Pulls of the Celestial Feminine

-Ned the Learnéd Seal

'Tis no mischance our hero should be moth-ish.
Drawn to circum the silver orb

wherein dwells the serpent with hawk's head
that bears the charge of his illumination—

not of night's shroud, but of our own fantasy
conceived in the fire and quickened by the breath

of the moon dragon, as evidenced during an eclipse,
when all imagination ceases function.

> *[Ned looks expectantly*
> *at a bucket of putrid fish]*

With the power to shift oceans,
why would she not also pull our blood?

Let it ebb and pulse to her design. Such things cause
not just distemper, but rickets and syphilis.

She lives in the whorl and magnet: the twisting
stew of particles and light that travel

cross epochs of space to compose a singular
being meant to stand naked before another

and say, *this is what we are*, a simple collection of—

> *[Ned balances an empty bottle, then*
> *flings it against a far wall to shatter]*

I implored Barnum to ride Elijah's chariot
to the lunar realm, as Astolfo did for Orlando,

and recover our Automate's wits, but he laughed
a bellyful and called a boy to clean my sick.

Love be madness and madness, lunacy. Still,
I wonder if our hero hasn't been right all along.

The One-Eyed Girl winks her gentle crescent
at the ides, as if to ask: Why would he search elsewhere?

Natural philosophers impart, all things lost on Earth
reappear, eventually, in the moon's spacious vale.

Outskirt

From the long view, the wetlands stun me—

                 patches of long grass sway

like dauphinesses lost in a troubadour's voice.

But up close, Mademoiselle,
                  the green is sickly:

old tire and gnarled rust protrude,
       orphan shrubs of oil and mud.

I lay in it anyway,
             for a little while,

feel the softness of earth.

Once the One-Eyed Girl whispered a story.

She found a garden behind a tenement,
       a small garden with a few sad carrots.

She lay among them and covered her face with soil,

then planted a single seed
             above her socket.

As she spoke, her blushing impelled me

to draw her a ship.

I hoped she understood I meant to take her away
one day, away

from this soot-black city
of regret and excrement

to a fertile land where from every branch,

like fattened fruit, hangs a single green eye.

Broadway & Ann

Curiosity wins in the underground—

                        Tunnels serpentine, electricity,
occasional unnatural liquid—

Too much to bear in my so-long city.

At first surface, I keep in shadow, but people

                        throng with such grace,
a starling's murmur twisting

at the behest of light.
Chaotic coordination,
I cannot help but join

and walk openly among them.

Focused on their gadgets,
no one notices just another synthetic boy
in his own 19th century,

enthralled by every last one of them:

their hair of colors and lengths; skin dappled, smooth,
or freckled; every eye, liquid and light.

                        The Chinese believe when a tiger dies,
                        her eyes sink into the earth
                                  to become amber,

but death is not necessary for us.
We are already compressed light—

Infinite procession to the mouth
of a hulking bridge.

Then absence becomes

      a poignant delicatessen, filled
      with a few unattended bottles,
      mustard hardening in the window.

No horses, banners, wood,
No trace—she, me, never here.

A Hundred Months, A Hundred Years, 1863

She received a letter on Thanksgiving,
scrawled almost illegibly
by a Lieutenant learning to use his left.

From that point on, as she dusted
the exhibit shelves
             or hurried the gawkers,

her eye would suddenly well up without warning.

All of us—Ned, Feejee, the whales—had no idea
how to give comfort.
             The dog who ran the loom growled in his sleep.

She told us she had a twin
                           who could pass.

Adamant to join the Union, he snuck
into Pennsylvania, enlisted in Lancaster,

and took a Minié ball to the throat
during the first day of Chickamauga.

In the ensuing silence, one of the whales
began a guttural knocking, setting tempo and beat.

The other let loose a melody.
Sharp ethereal whistle.
                    A piercing dirge.

In that way, they sung her favorite song:

A hundred months have passed, Lorena,
Since last I held that hand in mine,
And felt the pulse beat fast, Lorena,
Though mine beat faster far than thine.

The others joined, and the chorus filled the museum,
                    filtering to the street outside

where passersby stopped and searched
for the source of such

                        uncanny music.

Confused, I thought they were fashioning
a *miroir aux alouettes*
to keep her distracted,

                but my One-Eyed Girl
                is much too clever a lark for cages.

Looking back over fire and confinement,
I realize I hadn't yet learned to grieve.

Honey

Feejee Mermaid, Monkey Half

Claim octoroon, that's what I told her.

They'll be kinder,
        imagine you into a master's daughter.

Put the taste of money on their tongues.

She slapped me.

The fish—he fucking laughed.
                He never laughs.
But I care about safety.
                Every day she leaves
for Paradise Square,
looking for her mother in the market,

but the market is brass-knuckled,
is bread balled in the mouth,
                then spit in rows.

The market demands daily sacrifice
                to quell its rage,
strung up for all to see—

No city loves the South like New York,

so say the corpses at the pier, each one candled,
wax dripping on their chests.

Higher Law

Feejee Mermaid, Fish Half

For what have we gathered, this congress of oddities,
these natural rivals thrust together in a hall
of skulls and taxidermy badgers? What for, but to advise
our One-Eyed Girl. In our blind valley, she reigns.

In our sawdust palace, only she seems in tune
with the better angels; their choir hymning the great
schism outside: blue and grey rent by a cavalry saber
and grapeshot wasps. Her bonnie lies over the ocean;

her brother lies in Tennessee, yet here a fat shadow
carnival barks by day in the vestibule and haunts
back staircases at night. There must be some directive,
some divine order to explain the length of a war year,

how it curves around itself and seems to begin again.
Elsewise, this means nothing. Let the shadow be smitten,
let it have no quarter here. A conflagration's coming,
for the shadow may be brought low only when a light
burns bright enough to extinguish.

The Night of the Fire, Part 2, 1865

The shrieks mostly came from the street below
as the Kangaroo leapt from the fourth floor

like Greek fire shot from a catapult to Broadway
where a Union garrison awaited to put us down.

I heard boys call for blubber as my friends, the whales,
boiled. Ned, by their tank, pleading for rescue.

So many people clutched whatever they could carry:
gemstones, mementos, sequined costumes.

The Fat Lady collapsed from heat and two firemen
rolled her down the stairs. I watched,

unable to rise from my drawing table
as the smoke grew thicker. Then she was there.

The One-Eyed Girl yanked at me,
but I wouldn't budge, so she opened the box

and began to remove brass gear after brass gear.
Wracked with coughs and sweating,

she disassembled me and took me to the street, piece
by piece, to lie idle while the firemen laughed

behind cigarettes they lit with the flames. Barnum
was there too, trickle of blood down his cheek.

He blustered like a bull walrus at the police,
picking up whatever he could find, shoving it into crates.

When he came for me, I caught one last glimpse
of the One-Eyed Girl charging back

into the menacing black maw of collapsing wood,
then my head felt air before it landed with the rest of me.

I saw Barnum's face, red and sweating, as he closed
the crate's lid, and began hammering nails, one by one.

Stretching Cosmological Space

-The Dog who Ran the Loom

What can be said about time that hasn't
been said time after time? How it heals
all wounds, but waits for no man who's always
looking for ways to kill it while time without
mercy kills him and everyone he loves.
The duality's a sign of the times.
I spend every day watching the sand fall,
begging gravity to pull it faster,
but live in abject fear of the day
I'm out of grains. But our automaton's
unbound. He's ageless, so where does he get
his motivation? Why pursue when you
can only watch her become soil and dross?
Why play when there's nothing to win but loss?

Resurrection of the Eternal Boy

I don't understand why
these modern crowds gasp
at a sketched clipper or swan

when the automobile exists
                              and the airplane.

These people, hatless and strange,
pass the constant whir of dynamos,
            a blur of gear and illumined bronze,

as if it were *nothing*.

Men and woman sleeping in an aluminum albatross,
                  trailing smoke across the sky.

In such contrast with the stoic presence
            of broken colossi
            on the outskirts of gray cities
            as I trek northward.

Before my long slumber,
these structures were new
and churning out textiles, telegraph wire—

The irrepressible dream of a young nation,

inconceivable progress
                              now gutted,

the wild valley's reclamation project.

I emerged, half Van Winkled,
from a dusty crate left on the steps
of the Franklin.

             New city, new century,

my parts in a pile with only a Post-It
that read,
             Donation.

For years, I was a jigsaw
of limb and gear.

A man like my father, hunched
over a workbench,
                  trial and error.

Convalescence on a warehouse shelf
until my hand scratched its familiar lines.

Once finished, my new masters
displayed me.

At night, I discovered my legs
and devoured stray broadsheets stolen
from the nearby waste receptacle
before the janitor made his rounds.

The Young Gardener and the Fish's Word, Part 2

- The Fortune Teller

The villagers believed the fisherman and his birds washed out to sea. For days and nights, the young woman would not leave her bed—her grief bloomed into fever. The villagers fretted and paced the levee, wagging their fingers at the raging sun, fearing the loss of not one but two of their shiny young ones. They lamented under breath the lack of strawberries and fish. Until the sixth day, when the young woman awoke early in the morning to a sound. A sound on the verge of recognition but resistant to place. A sound like an old man's laugh, a halting guttural squawk. She rose from her bed and went to her garden, and on the earth lay an exhausted cormorant. As she approached, it lifted its head, met her gaze, and coughed up a fish, which flopped to life on a bed of pebbles. Its scales seemed familiar, so she picked it up and held it to her ear, where it croaked a single word only she could hear. She placed the fish in a porcelain bowl with a single berry floating on a lotus blossom. After dark, she walked to the mouth of the river, holding a lit candle. She stood perfectly still as the stars moved across the sky, and remained unmoved when the sun awoke in a tantrum. The villagers tittered, wondering if her grief had bloomed into not just fever, but madness.

Wild Overtakes Him

I used to sleep just out of sight of interstates.

The rhythm of cars calms me,
                                    recalls the ocean,
a deep hollow breath—
long, slow inhale, then a rush of air.

By day, I tear away the remaining red satin
of my waistcoat
                         and scream bare-breasted into the cold.

I search for anthills
                  to scatter,

and marten dens
                  to collapse.

They bear my wrath as I move north,
                        mile after mile.

The landscape also grows dramatic: hills give way
                      to green and gray peaks.
When twilight wraps its shroud around the conifers,
her glow appears above,

            and I am restored briefly to discover
the nearest bed of moss
            where restless sleep surveys the wreckage.

Last night, all night,
I heard the foliage bristle.
                        Some unseen beast hunts me.

Election Day, 1864

In prior quadrennials,
                    partisans milled about the green,

tapping barrel after barrel. The square
                            became an open-air tavern.

Men brawled and sang, undercards for the final tally;
then the Metropolitan police would line up,

knuckle dusters popping their palms,
truncheons twirling.
                        They'd advance like a scythe

until enough sots bloodied the dust,
                            and the mob dispersed.

This year, however, the men shuffle,
idly tugging on cuffs in the eerie silence.

The One-Eyed Girl returned from the street,
            said she saw Beast Butler striding about,
            chest puffed, every part of his face—
            eyes, mustache, chin—sagging like a hound.

He and his 5,000 men deployed in response
                to rumors of mayhem:
                saboteurs and copperheads

inbound from Canada, bent on depriving
the Railsplitter of his sheepish supporters.

The Democrats grumble about tyranny
                        until someone strikes
                        a calcium light,

a hissing star shining McClellan the victor
in all five boroughs, mollifying the Democrats,
so—Merciful Lord!—there's finally some sound:

a boisterous brass band clamors *Dixie*
as everyone heads home,
                              or at least indoors.

                    Tension finally cut,
I beg the whales to harmonize, hoping
the festive air will prove contagious,

                    but the One-Eyed Girl silences me,
                    withering a stare.

"One day,' she said, "Every part of me
will be enfranchised."

Attack!

Aroused from fitful
incubi of flickering
orange and the scent
of hot ambergris
emanating from the whale pool,
it takes some time
before I realize
I am not in the museum,
but the future:

a fairy tale
forest far in the North.
Then the beast bursts
forth from the underbrush.
I warn. I shout:

I say to you, Beast!
I am the thing itself,
but you must not touch me!
Within me lies the seed
of all animals, herbs and ores!

I grab
hold of an ear
and tear.
The beast clamps
its jaws on my arm
and maniacally shakes.
We roll
in the soft soil,
creating hillocks
on either side.
I dig in
until I feel separation,
a cold gust
through my shoulder.
I turn to see
the beast loping
away with its prize:

My own hand
waving goodbye.

On Faith Lost in Comely Settings

Diminished mountain, stone runneled weather,
       I'm there at the foot
       beneath a tartan of leaves.
       Can you see me?

The sun threads cumulo-mammoths
for the last go-around, last conflagration,
then age ushers in complex grays.

Autumn's a season for the young—
such colors flushed in the forest's irritating
titter. Desperate rodents hoard,
and hinds in the rut.

           Not a subtle season.

A pair of otters chase each other
through the shallow stream, and I watch
as long as I can, silent and hidden.

I want to play too, innocent, alive, and later
safe in some earthen den,

       but what puts the lonely in us?

Old mountain—ever shrinking,
with a reservoir for some far-off city
snaking around its base—impatient
       yet still,
       a touch of the waning
           devil-may-care.

Some seek, some are found,
but more are simply lost.

It takes one to know a lost one,
and you are not one.

Lake Champlain

On the edge of town, villagers whisper
about a monster in the deep, an elusive silver spark,
ancient and twice the length of a man.

They speak of skin hard as bone, sharp ridges
able to carve valleys through meat.

Rare that such good fortune befalls me,
that my course led me so near the realm

of Proteus, the shepherd of the seas
of which the sailors spoke so long ago.

I steal on to a trawler at dusk and listen
to rough boatmen bemoan the dwindling whitefish

as they pull up nets full of lamprey,
squirming flesh without a feature
but their razor-rimmed mouths.

These must be his minions, tasked
with sucking dry all who approach.

Then against the dying orange light,
he breaks the surface. Proteus,

fully airborne for a moment, before
plunging again.

Immediately, I dive and, without thought,
swim for my quarry. Deeper and deeper
into the frigid dark. My joints stiffen,

but still I swim until after what seems
ages, I grasp a fistful of mud.

At the bottom, I reconsider and swim aimless,
near blind with only a hint of light lost down here
from the distant surface.

Then a large shadow passes directly above.
With a violent lunge, I snatch at the shape
and feel my fist enclose a sharp whisker.

Startled, my adversary thrashes, but I hold fast.
O how he bucks and shudders, before propelling
upward! The water's cold resistance tries

to wrench me from his bony beard,
but I do not need to overpower him,
only to hold him long enough.

Together we breach under the pale light
of the One-Eyed Girl, who has risen to watch our battle.

We are eye to eye in the air, Proteus and me,
locked in an almost kiss.

And then we plunge again, back to the bottom.
For days we scuffle, hour after hour,
from surface to floor.

The One-Eyed Girl leaves and returns when she can
because she knows I struggle only for her.

When at the peak of my exhaustion,
 his skeletal face stills.

I can see him clearly now.
A spade-like snout. His eyes,
glassy marbles filled with molten copper.

I attempt to speak to him but can only think:
How do I reach her? I ask. *How do I reach her*
when she seems so far away?

From somewhere in the water,
from somewhere in my head,
a voice whispers:

Meet her in a circle, square it,
and then place it in a triangle.

Once you circle it again,
you will merge into androgyny.
Only then will your journey end.

Dreams Maybe Visions

-Ned the Learnéd Seal

The One-Eyed Girl arrived shaken one morning,
poor thing wan as a specimen bone, clearly phlegmatic.

I recommended an immediate course of vigorous
calisthenics and lamb shank, but she just petted my nose,

said she'd only suffered a startle, a vivid dream
around dawn. Despite my concern that her sudden fright
may harbinger more serious confection, I humored her.

> *[Ned clambers to the top of a tall stack
> of leather-bound books]*

I asked if her dream contained a flaming tetragrammaton
as to firmify my suspicion of her preciousness.

I thought her single clear eye could see so much more
than she let on, like the gentle horse-dung heat

of planets, falling into linear harmony
with vital organs, and elements.

Jupiter—Liver—Copper, or is it Tin?
Venus—Kidney—Copper.

Holy trinities, or virtuosic trios plucking celestial strings
in realms too small for the eyes of Barnum,
but not *this* seal! This seal can see.

> *[Ned selects a tome with many medieval
> etchings and leafs through]*

Instead she described something more vexing: A man
with a sun for a head, aggressively posed,
while a moon-faced woman points and laughs

at Chanticleer chasing a hen round a giant black egg.
I oohed as she spoke and promised to consult the lore,
but I already knew what this abode.

He will come for her soon. Too long has Barnum's
watery gaze shadowed her movements—each angle of
knee, each arc of wrist.

For her sake, for our sake, pray that as with energy
and money, the accounts of love are strictly balanced.

The Last Whistle-Stop Tour, 1865

The city washed in fireworks for six days,
                                    red and gold
absolving the revelers
around bonfires
                in every square.

The One-Eyed Girl described it as American Beltane,

a primal exhale after years
            fraught with the tight faces of strangers.

But when the news of April fifteenth arrived
on the wire, the fires were immediately
                                    extinguished.

By morning, black crepe
draped every window.

For nine days, this hypocrite city tore open its garments,
                                    beat its breast
like the most professional of mourners.

The performance climaxed with a funeral
procession 160,000 strong.

The One-Eyed Girl said she'd followed alongside
the two-hundred freedmen
                who took up the rear,
                allowed to march at the last minute
                by order of Secretary Stanton.

The police provided escort to prevent
any harassment, but none occurred.

Instead, the same men who lynched
Black men in the street during the riots
                              now applauded,
                              cheered their support.

"Strange that this gives me hope,"
The One-Eyed Girl mumbled,
as if maybe things could finally get better,

                              but the hope was short-lived.

When the freedmen reached the site of the Catafalque,
            it had already been dismantled—

Lincoln loaded on the train bound for Albany.

Black Fly Rain

-Feejee Mermaid, Monkey Half

See them boots,
                   freshly shined,

flat on the sawdust boards of privies.

Grinning balloons with Xed-out
eyes groaning satisfied

through the crescent portholes
of cartoon shacks.

From birth, American boys learn
                                to expand,

three piece suits and derbies
                     spreading their legs

on westward trains, gold watch chains

across their guts hold back
                 pounds of corn and steak.

Red-faced boys blustering for timber,
oil, and iron,

every single one a Baron
                    of the Rockies

entitled to put a bullet in anything
                   with hair: Animal or man

pooling black in the dust.
         Best not to struggle, let 'em have their fill.

Green Mountain Boy

Olive. Mint. Hunter. Lime.
Olive. Hunter. Mantis. Lime.

       The sunless light enables the innumerable
       New England hues.

They all seem so drab in comparison to her eye,
                        who visits nightly.

Real men are liquid, feckless,

and all are dangerous
no matter how much perfume and pomade.

Each one lives on the verge of frenzy,
ready to gnash and ravage.

A frozen flood of words cascades
through the gorge.

Static violence,
                trapped in a moment.

A bluish white photograph of what happened,
what I can never forget.

I watched him dissemble for decades,
                    all teeth and charm.

I hear you Barnum, your cynical voice
                  still barking.
I feel the end of your endless
              carnival pitch approach.

Everything that Has Happened Will Happen

In this narrow pass,
                    the wind shrieks
and beats a chaotic retreat
                    from the looming anvil.

Granite rises on either side.
Crags peak and valley like petrified ocean.

I peer through copses of deciduous—
winter-stripped, now a capillary thicket
                            darkened by black blood.
Life abandoned ship long ago.

I can't help but write the same lyric,
                    a circular desire that collapses
                    onto itself into a single point

before expanding outward again.
                            It never gets better.
                            It just repeats.

On one of the cliffs, a face appears,
an ancient man with a prominent nose and brow.

I move toward the foot of the slope, hoping to ascend
and receive advice,

but no sooner do I begin, a blinding crack atomizes
the air—a deafening flash—

                    the face slides then separates
                    into caroming rock.

I stumble back. Boulders narrowly miss on either side.
One comes to a stop in front of me.
It resembles an eye.

I take a moment to check myself,
see if everything's intact,

only to be surprised by the damage
my journey has inflicted:

            missing arm; painted face chipped
and faded by sun; metal joints corroding;

hope's delicate geography turning treacherous—

I have lost all sense of direction,
no compass to guide me
except one heavenly body.

Saturnine Night

-Ned the Learnéd Seal

They came again
when the sun was at its highest. Kayaks
covered with the skin of our siblings.
The dull obsidian, glinted wet.

The harpoons shone as well.
They made an etheric whistle en route,
last song to pierce the chest, a measured
étude—the eschatology of seal-ness.

[*Ned sits perfectly still on a plaster rock,
flanked by a purple velvet curtain.*]

Panic pervaded the colony; slick bodies
flopped this way and that in search
of the shortest path to the cobalt sanctuary
of the deep. During the chaos,

I lost my pup. Her bark, distinct and distressed,
rang through the clamor, but the stampede
carried me farther away until we were corralled.
Hunters suddenly on all sides. I was struck—

[*Ned raises flippers, covers eyes, remains
silent for several long moments.*]

I awoke to his beardless mouth pulled back,
revealing his teeth. He said he'd chosen me
because I was the prettiest. He said he intended
to teach me so many things, and if I learned well
and earned well, he'd restore my pup to me.

Then, Barnum named me Ned, and I
was made a boy-seal, for no one would believe
a girl-seal to be learnéd, and, besides,
it's not like the patrons are checking parts.

> [*Ned turns her back to the audience revealing
> a web of scars, previously invisible.*]

After many years of impressing the masses
with pinnepedian ingénuity, I'm beginning
to suspect he never had her, my pup. He left
her flayed carcass glittering on the rocks.

Our One-Eyed Girl knows loss too:
her brother, battle-slain; her mother,
in search of work, now three years
gone. I dissolved to tell her my tale,

in hopes we may reach a mutual symphony
of sorts. Two more damaged remnants
abiding our messianic time.

Beastly Denouements//The Night of the Fire, Part 1, 1865

The low snarls rumble, muscling
in on fitful slumber. I awake in a slow

struggle from dream to nothing
but bituminous trees—the supremacy

of black on black, without even
her pale eye to guide me.

> //
>
>She swept the floor in languid arcs,
>collecting the tracked detritus
>
>of another long day, humming
>softly to the accompaniment
>
>of Ned's flapping snore. I, at my desk,
>as always, composing.

My foggish thoughts take moments
to crystallize. The growl is not nightmare,

but reality. Blind to my surroundings,
I attempt to locate its source by ear alone,

But my pulse alla marcia (I have a pulse!?)
pounds a thick bass inside my head.

> //
>
>The room lit by a few oil lanterns
>set low, a honeyed glow for our closing
>
>rituals, but the stairs to the floor below
>lay dark, so we heard him first. The familiar
>
>thump of a heavy man trying to walk
>gentler than his body would allow.

I fugue into the brush, but my lack
of caution betrays me, for I only make it

fifteen paces or so before colliding
with something solid. Knocked back.

So few moments before the beast
strikes, I scramble for any passable weapon.

> //
> He was only a shaded mass behind his lantern
> as he ascended the stairs. I shot a glance
>
> at my One-Eyed Girl. She had stopped
> her sweeping and seemed to be scanning
>
> the room, taking inventory of the shelves,
> the curios, and jarred rows of fetal oddities.

An infinite pause—then its full weight
drives me prostrate into the earth.

The beast's breath, ragged and hot
on my neck. It bites once, then twice,

but I'm made of harder stuff than flesh.
Baffled, it relents for an instant.

> //
> He set his lantern on my desk at the head
> of my parchment. Its light blinded me,
>
> but I heard him purr, *we've danced for too long,
> my little rum blowen.* His steps quickened
>
> toward her. Then a shatter, and the acrid
> waft of alcohol, another jar followed the first.

Momentary space. I thrust my elbow
up and back, catching it full on its snout.

Stunned for an instant, the beast lifts its weight.
I flip over and raise a knee into its belly,

stealing air, raising it off the ground.
My lone hand gropes in the darkness.

                                        //
                    She must have hit him at least once
                    because I heard him grunt. His voice,

                        its famous mellifluousness, grew serrated
                        as he demanded her peace. But she fought.

                        I saw them as shadows over the lantern,
                        monstrous and thrashing across the wall.

The beast recovers and sets upon my torso,
opening gash after gash to be filled

with steaming saliva. Then my hand
seizes its quarry, a heavy stone.

With all strength left, I bring it down
on skull, feel the bone shudder and give.

                                        //
                    I, whose movements remained confined
                    to a creator's program, sat helpless

                        as she struggled. At one point, he shrieked,
                        sounding indignant. His shadow doubled

                        its efforts. I stared into the lantern before me,
                        that empty between wick and flame.

A yelp trails to whimper, I bring
the stone down again and again,

until the beast lies motionless atop me.
I drop the stone, and run my hand

through its thick fur, surprised by its
softness, then nothing—

                              //
                    Then something happened. My arm,
                    previously reserved for poem and sketch,

                    felt a sudden warmth—filled with the fire
                    before it. I suddenly flexed elbow, wrist,

                    reached out and struck the lantern. It flew
                    across the room and exploded, igniting
                    the alcohol-soaked floor.

Belief or Remembrance

-The One-Eyed Girl

Barnum's lucky.

I had hold of a four inch dagger of glass,
was making to slash his bread bag—

I would've hanged for it,
but there's no way he puts
his poxy william in me unscathed.

Regardless, I hear him bellowing
all the way down Broadway.

Calling for the fire wagon to save
his precious collection.

I stood there for a moment watching the young fire
sway like General George Lushington.

I was tempted to let the whole museum
and everything in it turn to ash

soft enough to ride the wind
back across the Atlantic.

After all, this whole enterprise was conceived
to bilk goosecaps and simons of a hard day's pay.

It would be just desserts. Yet I couldn't shake
the feeling that, over Barnum's shoulder,

I saw the mechanical kid swat that lantern.

He had only ever come to life to sketch
a few birds and winged babies, maybe a poem
in foreign script, all fancy and looped.

I'd chatter at him after closing
to ease the loneliness, at least he *resembled*

another person, but I never imagined
him listenin'. But once Barnum
finished his tumble, I looked the boy

in his painted eye, searching for some spark.

Then I saw it—

Time stopped. The flames froze
into blossoms of garnet, ruby, and gold.

Time does not pass. It's ever fixed.

Us people, and our tribulations,
simply pass through it,

but not this strange mechanical boy.

In that instant, I realized everything I love *lives* here,

a motley collection of souls
compiled through kidnapping or coercion;
foolish dreams; even experimental surgery.

I lived looking over my shoulder
in a building built of sucker and hoax.

If it weren't for these creatures
who I imagined sang
when my brother died—

The seal. The whales. The dog.
That eerie fish-monkey.
I couldn't let them burn.

Among the crystalline crags of fire,
I flew to his desk, wrenched open the back,

stacked brass, and hauled what I
could to the street.

Floorboards and stairs
seemed to float mid-collapse,

but they held me, remaining
cool under my feet.

On the seventh trip, I carried the boy.
I left him in safety with a mother's kiss,
promising return.

Then back in through the black smoke
that seemed as fixed as a distant storm.

I searched for the others until I noticed
something else moving.

Not the flames, or the falling wreckage of history,
but the dog who ran the loom

racing back and forth in his corner,
working as frantic as me.

I approached, and I'm not sure
if this next part is remembrance or belief,

but I saw him weaving a tapestry
of the finest silk, unburnt, not even touched by soot.

The story it told is this one you read,
and then the American Museum collapsed into itself.

Homily

-Feejee Mermaid, Fish Half

If we break every yoke, if we let loose
every spirit from thralldom,
their light shall break forth as the morning.

So sayeth Isaiah, yet bitterness and death fount
in ever fresh streams. Our world lurches forward
painfully, a caisson crossing yesterday's battleground.

Its wheels sink in the sodden earth, emerge bloodstained,
go around again, but eventually another meadow
reached, free of iron and bone.

Our factories and shops abound in ruthless economy.
The wealthy and working tramp through these rooms—
their faces grotesquely average—

and beneath the clicking of hobnail, those who came
before fused in a writhing flail of torment like glass
in a whirlwind, each individual scratch insignificant,

but together—death by a thousand cuts.
Together—A history of boot and face.
Our light *wants* to break forth as mourning,

but the past is a singular cataclysm.
It leaves rubble, stretching further skyward.
Our One-Eyed Angel faces it. She wants to stay,

but the volcanic wind blows her
to a future she'll never see.

The Young Gardener and the Fish's Word, Part 3

-The Fortune Teller

As the third night fell, darker than the last, the
young woman kept her vigil alone until a small girl
named Etsuko brought her another candle. The two of
them stood perfectly still until, one by one, each of the
villagers joined them (except Daichi who was sick from
eating a spoiled pear), each lighting a candle from the
last. When the whole village was assembled, a gentle
glow arose on the horizon, a serene sun the young man
could see in the blackest night. He turned toward it and
headed home, his boat heavy with fish.

You see, Poppet, love tethers us
to the things of this world. Thousands
of candles will light off a single flame,
while the life of the first will not shorten.
Happiness only increases when shared.
If an object you ardently pursue brings little,
remember most pleasure springs from the unexpected.

History-ish

-The Dog who ran the Loom

What's left when all is stripped away? No need
to feed, sleep, or bathe—just a pure plastic
existence, a few firing synapses
and senseless awe. Is there still love
in some purer form without the need to ram
into one another? Or is love in all forms
a desire to consume and be validated,
to grow fat on the heart of the other
before you're eaten from the inside.
The Automaton knows nothing of love,
but still he pursues a memory. Maybe
memory is all he is and ever was,
a record etched in brass and spun over
and over, but then again, maybe not.

Mount Washington

Near the summit, the gales begin to slash
                              from every cardinal point.

Snowflakes whip in atypical directions,

unclear whether they fall from sky
or spring whole from the earth.

Suddenly, the clouds part above,

              and she is there.

Too cold for real boys, but I am warm
                              because she is close.

From the highest rock, I stretch
my remaining arm until the metal joint buckles.

But my hand closes on nothing but snowflakes.

They sit on my palm without even the courtesy to melt.

Night-mountain, lonely peak
              surrounded by un-seeable valleys.

No closer, she is no closer.

Perhaps, up there is not our world,
                              but another,
where we can neither speak, nor touch,

a world behind glass like my exhibit back home.

Perhaps, our last thought, if it is true, echoes
into the ether where it remains

a repeated gesture of impeccable grace,
a perfect grand jeté.

Then, below me, I see it:
                                        A single light
like a beacon on some distant shore.
It flickers alone for a moment,
                                        then multiplies

until the horizon brightens
under the dark powder of an absent sun.

-Ecrit par L'Automate de Maillardet

Notes

L'Automate de Maillardet

At the turn of the nineteenth century, Henri Maillardet, a skilled Swiss clockmaker living in London, constructed an automaton. As opposed to famous frauds like the Mechanical Turk, this figure of a young draughtsman at his desk proved genuine and possibly the most sophisticated machine of its time. Able to create four drawings and three poems, it was hailed as a marvel, a miracle machine. Maillardet's creation toured Europe, exhibiting as far as the Tsar's court in St. Petersburg. Its fame reached across the Atlantic, and the greatest American Impresario of the nineteenth century, P. T. Barnum, decided he must have it for his growing collection, so *L'Automate de Maillardet* voyaged to the United States.

From this point, the automaton's history grows murky. Not much exists in the historical record to track its whereabouts for the next century. It is believed that the machine eventually found its way into the collection of one of Barnum's museums where it was subsequently lost in a fire. In 1928, a donation was made to the Franklin Institute in Philadelphia. Among the contents of the donation was a strange crate filled with what looked like singed gears and mannequin parts. It took several years for Charles Roberts, a talented mechanic on the institute staff, to piece it together. Once Roberts was able to get it into working order, the museum realized they were in possession of Maillardet's lost automaton. The machine still resides in the Franklin where it was made the centerpiece of its own exhibit.

Timeline of Important Events

c. 1800 - Henri Maillardet constructs his Automaton.

c. 1834 - The Automaton comes to the United States.

1837 - The Automaton is first exhibited in Barnum's American Museum in New York City.

April 12th, 1861 - Confederate troops fire on Fort Sumter, ushering in the American Civil War.

July 4th, 1863 - The Union wins the battles of Gettysburg and Vicksburg, turning the tide of conflict; the One-Eyed Girl begins working at the American Museum.

November 8th, 1864 - Lincoln wins reelection over his former General, George McClelland.

April 15th, 1865 - Lincoln is assassinated.

July 13th, 1865 - Barnum's American Museum burns to the ground. The fire is believed to be the work of Confederate saboteurs.

November, 1928 - The remains of the Automaton are donated to the Franklin Institute in Philadelphia.

2007 - The Automaton becomes the centerpiece of his own exhibition at the Franklin Institute in Philadelphia.

About the Poems

IN THE FRANKLIN INSTITUTE refers to multiple drawings the automaton is capable of sketching, reproductions of which can be found on the website of the Franklin Institute.

SHE BLINKS, SHE MANIFESTS, 1863 makes use of the photographs of Matthew Brady from the Battle of Gettysburg.

ON FEVERS OF THE MELANCHOLIC AND THEIR DEMANDS owes a debt to *Passions and Tempers: a History of the Humours* (2007) by Noga Arikha. Language from this book was adapted concerning various remedies and the anecdote of the one-eyed kitchen wench.

CREATION II uses *Vocabulum; or, the Rogue's Lexicon* (1859) by George W. Matsell. Other poems in this book also make use of this resource, including: BELIEF OR REMEMBERANCE.

MYSTICAL PULLS OF THE CELESTIAL FEMININE adapts language and describes images from *Alchemy and Mysticism* by Alexander Roob (1997) and draws from *Orlando Furioso* by Ludovico Ariosto.

The title of BROADWAY & ANN refers to the original address of Barnum's American Museum.

The title and the italicized portion from A HUNDRED MONTHS, A HUNDRED YEARS, 1863 are lyrics from the song *Lorena* (1856), lyrics by Rev. Henry D.L. Webster.

HIGHER LAW takes its title from a William H. Seward speech from 1850.

THE NIGHT OF THE FIRE, PART 2, 1865 owes a debt to the account printed in the *New York Times* on July, 14th 1865.

ATTACK!: The italicized portion comes from *Conversation between Saturn and a chemist* (1706) as cited in *Alchemy and Mysticism* (1997) by Alexander Roob.

LAKE CHAMPLAIN owes a slight debt to the TV show *River Monsters* and also incorporates some material from *Alchemy and Mysticism* (1997) by Alexander Roob.

DREAMS MAYBE VISIONS incorporates language and describes images from *Alchemy and Mysticism* (1997) by Alexander Roob.

SATURNINE NIGHT makes a brief reference to Giorgio Agamben's *The Time That Remains*.

HOMILY adapts language from *The Blessings of Abolition: A Discourse delivered in the First Unitarian Church, Sunday July 1st 1860,* by W. H. Furness, Minister. This poem also makes reference to Walter Benjamin's *Theses on the Philosophy of History.*

The italicized portion at the end of THE YOUNG GARDENER AND THE FISH'S WORD, PART 3 adapts material from an actual fortune telling card written by an anonymous author. The machine also mildly electrocuted the author of this book.

Acknowledgements

I would like to express my gratitude to all the people who offered assistance and encouragement during the creation of this book, especially my family and friends without whom I could not achieve much. James & Judy Pennock, Michael & Amanda Pennock, and my nephew William. I would like to thank Erica Wright and Ricardo Maldonado who have been with this project since the beginning and have read every word multiple times. Your forbearance is epic. Thanks to other folks who read this book in manuscript form or gave encouragement: Davin Rosborough, Jason MacDougall, James Ellenberger, and Timothy Van Dyck.

I'd also like to show my appreciation for the good folks at the University of Cincinnati. Especially John Drury, Jim Cummins, and Philip Tsang who advised on this manuscript.

I'd like to thank Robert L. Giron and everyone at Gival Press for giving this book a chance to be in the world. I'd also like to thank C.M. Mayo for judging it acceptable.

So many others deserve acknowledgement: Lucia Gajda, Nick Gorski, Eric Hupe, Katie Knoll, Julie MacDougall, Emily Mitchell, Anjili Pal, Ondrej Pazdirek, Lidia Sek, Dario Sulzman, and Jared Szafman to name a few.

So many others, you know who you are.

Lastly, I'd like to thank the editors at *Gulf Coast: A Journal of Literature and Fine Arts* for publishing "Outskirt" and "Reprieve as Unlikely Baltimore" in more nascent forms.

About the Author

Matthew Pennock is the author of *Sudden Dog* (Alice James Books, 2012), which won the Kinereth-Gensler Award. As per the terms of that award, he joined the board of Alice James Books in 2011, In 2014, he co-created AJB's editorial board with executive editor Carey Salerno, and then became the board's first chairperson, a position he held until 2020. He received his MFA from Columbia University and his PhD from the University of Cincinnati. His poems have been widely published in such journals as *Gulf Coast, Denver Quarterly, Western Humanities Review, Guernica: A Magazine of Art and Politics, New York Quarterly, LIT*, and elsewhere. He currently owns and operates a learning center outside of Washington, D.C.

Photo by Amanda Pennock.

Poetry from Gival Press